...with the light on...

The art of *Alexandria Barrett*.

I tasked Alexandria with interpreting this book artistically and she in turn tasked me with placing her work where I thought appropriate. Her art definitely does the book justice, I only hope my placements return the favor.   ~CLG~

...with the light on...

(...and other life strategies)

Carl L. Gould

Writers Club Press
San Jose   New York   Lincoln   Shanghai

...with the light on...
(...and other life strategies)

All Rights Reserved © 2002 by MilestonesUnlimited,Inc.

No part of this book may be reproduced or transmitted in any form or by any means, graphic, electronic, or mechanical, including photocopying, recording, taping, or by any information storage retrieval system, without the permission in writing from the publisher.

Writers Club Press
an imprint of iUniverse, Inc.

For information address:
iUniverse, Inc.
5220 S. 16th St., Suite 200
Lincoln, NE 68512
www.iuniverse.com

The publisher, author, contributing authors and artists accept no responsibility or credit for any successes you experience due to the ideas and expressions contained in this book. You *must* accept and express your unique gifts yourself to their utmost potential and take full credit for the results you achieve!

ISBN: 0-595-23315-5

Printed in the United States of America

This book is dedicated to…

    my daughter who inspires me;

    and my son who reminds me everyday—
    of the boy I was, the man I am,
    and the person I hope to become someday.

    ~CLG~

Epigraph

❀

"*Your limitations are not imposed on you. They are accepted by you*"

<u>Ralph Marston</u>

"You are not limited to the life you now live.
It has been accepted by you as the best you can do at this time.
Any time you're ready to go beyond the limitations currently in your life, you're capable of doing that by choosing different thoughts."

asamanthinketh.net

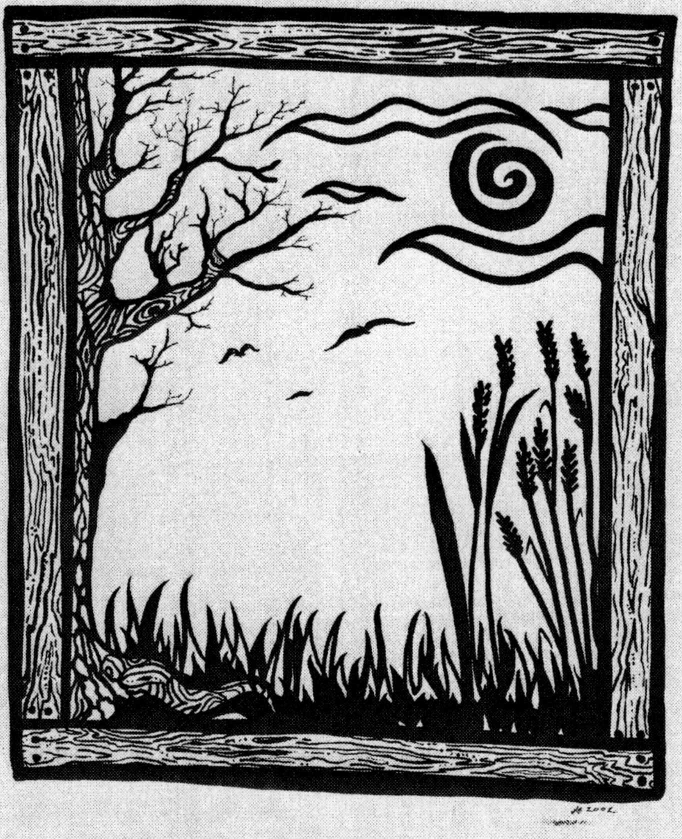

Contents

❦

Epigraph	vii
Foreword	xiii
List of Contributors	xv
Introduction: *"How It Came to Pass"*	xvii

"Holding Hands" 1
   Chapter 1: The Weans 3
   Chapter 2: The Teens 5
   Chapter 3: The Scenes 6
   Chapter 4: The Leans 8
   Chapter 5: The Means 10
   Chapter 6: …And finally 12

"The Rhyme…and the Ancient Mariner" 15
   Chapter 1: The Sea 17
   Chapter 2: The Wisdom 19
   Chapter 3: The Rhyme Created 21
   Chapter 4: The Sonnet Follows the Sea 23
   Chapter 5: High Tide 25
   Chapter 6: Low Tide 27
   Chapter 7: Ebb and Flow 29

Chapter 8: Charting The Course 31
Chapter 9: The End 33

Illustrations : ...*a poetic compilation* 35
  "Bue Hue" 37
  "A Passage" 39
  'Wedge' 40
  'Vision' 42
  'Albatross' 44
  'Shutter' 46
  'M.O.' 47
  "I'll take...that one." 48
  'Wealth' 49
  'Conscience' 51
  'Blue eyes, blue skies' 52
  "Fracture" 53
  'White Water' 55
  "Naesman" 57
  'Zenpen' 58
  'Clouds Roll By' 59
  "Braveheart" 61
  "Vicarious" 62
  'Olive' 64
  'Gale' 65
  "Twinge" 67
  "Weightless" 69
  "Till Then" 70
  "The Search" 72
  "A Coming Out" 74
  "And Whence a Storm" 76
  Coyotes Dating 77
  'Union' 79

"Cloak" 80
"Ode to Security" 82
"On the Fence" 83
"Through a Looking Glass" 85
"A Moment in Time" 87
'Gladiator' 88
'The Giving Tree' 89
"Cube" 90
"Ed" 92
Sometime/Somewhere 94
"Author" 95
"On Your Shoulder" 96
"Survival" 97
"I hope you were paying attention" 98
"The Continuing Paradox of Paradise" 100
"A Familiar Look" 102
"Scared and Running". 103

"Ripples on the Shore" 105
   Chapter 1: Alone? I Dream… 107
   Chapter 2: Fracture! Free from the Ledge. 109
   Chapter 3: Sending the Signal (I want to be gathered!) 114
   Chapter 4: That Special Stone 116
   Chapter 5: "Daddy, I'm thirsty!" 118
   Chapter 6: At the Shoreline. 120
   Chapter 7: Tossed Into the Water (Make a Wish!) 123
   Chapter 8: Under the Water. Now what? 128
   Chapter 9: I Glow; I Know 130
   Chapter 10: Tossing a Stone Each Day 133
   Chapter 11: The Beginning… 134
Afterword 135

Foreword

❀

"If You Insist…"
One evening when Carl was at his sister Michele's place, he read a rather rough and never-completed book of poems and short stories. Upon reading this and doing some internal searching, he realized that he had held up years of ideas and thoughts and feelings with no clear avenue to express them. He began to write. Some three years later; "…with the light on."

If you insist I can tell you the stories that brought Carl to this place today.
If you insist I can tell you of a young man with a cast on his leg walking a mile uphill to work.
If you insist I can tell you of a wife, a daughter, a son.
If you insist I can speak of ten brothers and sisters.
If you insist I.

One evening when Carl was at his sister Michele's place, he read a rather rough and never-completed book of poems and short stories. Upon reading this and doing some internal searching, he realized that he had held up years of ideas and thoughts and feelings with no clear avenue to express them. He began to write. I was surprised to learn the rough and never completed book was mine.

Today's world does not always allow for the space and freedom to extend beyond your everyday obligations of work and family. When that time can happen new ideas and worlds are explored. Those things that we see everyday are absorbed and added to the landscape within our minds. Sometimes they are published for other people to read.

Thank You,
Ralph Gould ('Zendar')

List of Contributors

❀

Contributing Author:
Ralph S. Gould

Contributing Artist:
Artistically Interpreted by; Alexandria Barrett

Introduction

❦

"How It Came to Pass"

A lonely path
      That one must take
And forge the steps.
      Thy thoughts will make…

                I create the time
                To ink the word
                And make I rhyme
                As well it should…

Zenbue

"One Word, One War"

What word is this?
> You use my friend

For speak it not
> No means—no end.

I chose the same
> Tools different the task

Your word brings out
> No speak—my mask

I shutter–I think
> You print–in bold

My secret–it's safe
> In the story I've told

Why choose this word?
> My friend—no more

I speak it not
> For fear–I'm sure

Zenbue

So how did it come to pass?

If you told me that I would write a book containing poetry, I'd have said you were crazy. While I enjoy reading poetry somewhat, I never had any desire to pursue writing in that style. As a matter of fact, truth be told I don't really consider this poetry. I consider them short stories.

How this all came to pass is that I realized that I organize my thoughts in short and simple phrases. Another strategy I employ is to rhyme those phrases so they are easier to recall. While in the past I took this for a shortcoming and a challenge in maintaining focus, I decided to go with the flow a little bit and began capturing my ideas. I soon realized that this 'shortcoming' was in fact an outlet and another form of expression that allowed me to process all that is around me.

And in life's processes of questioning, exploring, growing, and navigating the seemingly infinite amount of experiences, information, and distractions—I sought a simple vehicle to help me filter out and funnel in that which keeps me on the path of life I choose. How'd you like that last sentence? Now do you see how important it is for me to keep things simple…☺?

These stories and poems have become simple formulas for dealing with situations and experiences in our lives. I chose to write them out in the form of stories because when shared, each person gets to interpret them and experience them in their own way; in a way that makes sense for you in your own lives.

I have written the poems and stories in a style that I call '3-dimensional'.

1st Dimension:
I have intentionally chosen words that have multiple meanings so that each poem and story reaches a fork in the road. Therein lies the life strategy....making decisions at critical times of your life. And what meaning you decide to attach to these experiences determines the quality of life you will lead. A singular experience can mean one thing to one person and something totally different to another—all depending on the meaning each person adds to that experience.

As an example, 3 people take a ride on a roller coaster. One person describes it as exhilarating, one as terrifying, the third gets sick to their stomach (so you know how that person would describe it ..☺). Same roller coaster, three different meanings, three different experiences. A critical times during that ride, each person chose a different meaning for the event. Therefore, each had a vastly different experience.

We all get to choose the meaning in every (yes, every) situation in our lives. May the stories enclosed offer you some options as to how to interpret present, past and future events in *your* life.

2nd Dimension:
I have arranged the lines of the poems in "Illustrations" visually to suggest the deeper meaning to that story. How often have you heard someone say something to you; and you just felt that there was more to what they were saying? Knowing the deeper meaning would reveal the person's true feelings, wouldn't it? **What is the story behind the story?**

3rd Dimension
Each poem and short and short story answers a question and asks another. It is through our constant questioning that we 'navigate' our lives, isn't it?

My simple formula for this book; and it's mission is this…

To learn—and share what I've learned.
To create—and be creative.
To grow—and empower others to pursue their own growth.

The poem, "How it came to pass", is just the story of applying what was once thought to be a weakness and turn it into a strength. While by no stretch of the imagination do I consider myself a poet, I do strongly believe in expressing that in which you believe ("One Word, One War").

Find what is empowering about any situation, and apply it constructively. Contribute to the big picture, the small picture; whatever picture—just contribute. If this is what I have to offer; so be it. And if my sharing this work adds any value to you in that direction, all the better.

So what is it for you??

What do you have to offer? Where do your talents lie?…. in thought?……in action?……in the spoken word?….in the written word?

So I offer you this collection of observations, of illustrations. And a challenge…allow yourself, for just a moment to identify (and accept) where your genius lie. Then express it. Go for it! There *is* a reason why you are inclined in that area. And while it may not be (or have been) exactly what you asked or hoped for, it is right.

It's right because it's right for you.

Begin to carve that path. Along that path are clues. Clues to the meaning; answers to that question. May this collection be one more stop along the way.

~CLG~

"Holding Hands"

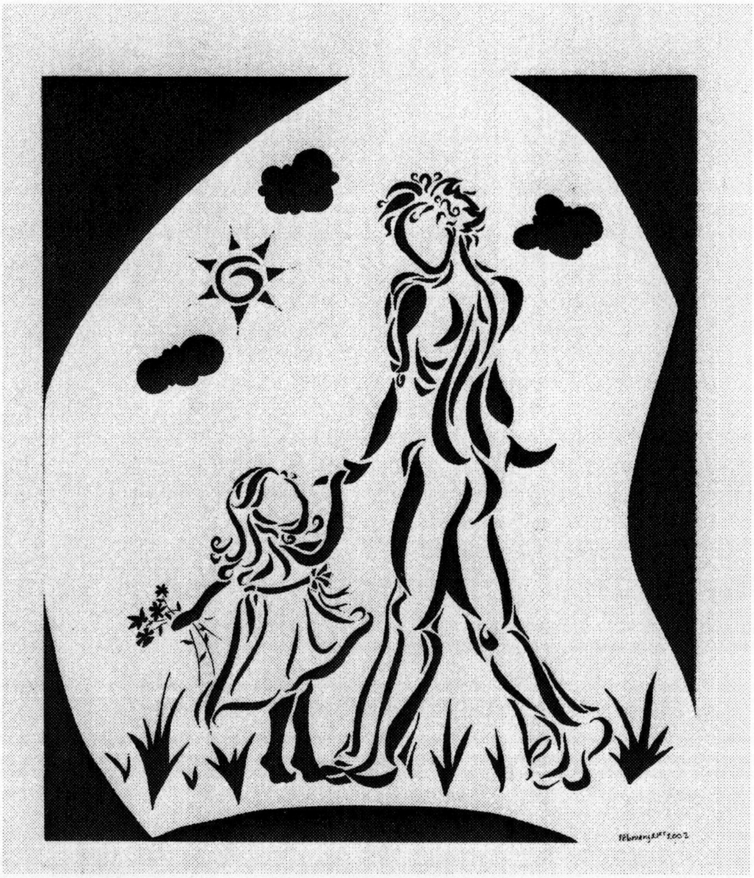

Chapter 1

❀

The Weans

Her fingers together
They hold onto one
Her heart—her soul
It warms the son

So full of life
Her energy abounds
We skip through the sand
Her feats astound.

My vision of life
It circles around
I'm blind to her past
A deafness of sound.

So many questions
I have of her quest
And my pride like the son
Exudes from my chest

*I am bound by my silence
These thoughts—mine alone
The answers to these—
In time they will show.*

*How far will she go?
How will she grow?
Who will kill and
Who will die to learn
What I already know?*

*This ray of light
Her print in the sand
And all the while...
We were holding hands...*

Chapter 2

The Teens

Stride for stride
Pace for pace
No line to cross
To win the race

A vision of beauty
And motion of grace
She gleams in the son
With barely a trace

Three/quarters to finish
And hardly a breath
She's come so far
In such a short test

Quicker than yore
Outpaces the man
And just as she passes…
…Let's go of my hand

Chapter 3

The Scenes

*In a movie I saw
As I viewed from afar
She who wrote a script
And became the star*

*My little girl
Who skipped in the sand
Curious about life
While holding my hand*

*Was now on her own
And making it reel
Her dreams came to life
For the world to sea*

*She scaled through walls
That no one could stand*

*The world could be found
…In the palm of her hand*

Chapter 4

❁

The Leans

*I've never seen
In all my years
A hummingbird
Reduced to tears*

*Scared and bruised
Short on breath
She bares the wait
Of the world she did test*

*I see in her eyes
The pain and the want
To cower away
And feel as though shunned*

*She chased her dream
The thrill of the run
The terrain at times rough
The obstacles—blunt*

*She returns to the race
But not just quite yet
Grasp a moment before
A chance to forget*

*For just this one time
With no one around
A tear down her cheek
Her spirit aground*

*Love sometimes tough
And never is fair
My wisdom to act
I cannot share*

*A gesture I know
To calm an old friend
To offer my heart…
…I reach out my hand.*

Chapter 5

The Means

It is through only one set of eyes
That a person must use
To tunnel through strife
In order to create—an extraordinary life

A specialty in deed
To peripheral the scene
And engulf the wisdom
Of an end to the means

To walk a mile
In another's shoes
You'll arrive a place
With a reluctant view

Though the scenery cloudy
And hindsight quite clear
I resist the temptation
To shelter the fear

*A mysterious method
Yet a way nonetheless
It's a part of some plan
For the best,…I guess*

*As tough my love
As soft my palm
My jaw clenched tight
Of her vision I'm drawn
To wait out the storm*

*All the while I pray
For her—safe home
As my heart extends…
…To ask on her own*

Chapter 6

❁

...And *finally*

Her head was down
Her energy low
I watch this take place
In the scenery below

Some laugh—
Some cry—
Some mourn the passing
Do they even know why?

He looks just like he
That silly little grin
As all of his life
Through eternity and then

He shared the secret
And dared not to speak

Of the gifts he brought
And left those beneath

Her gift stood proud
When it counted the most
All eyes turned to
This most gracious host

She lead them out
And by heart—to understand
To feel better of life
And live on as planned

With my fingers together
And my toes in the sand
I begin my new life…

…And we were holding hands

*"The Rhyme...
...and the Ancient Mariner"*

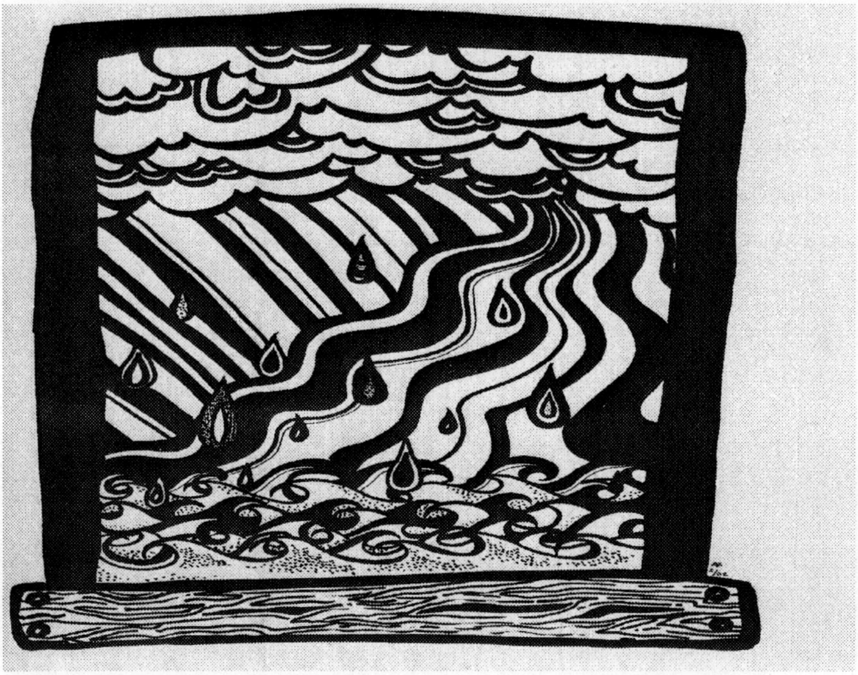

Chapter 1

❧

The Sea

The water that washes on shore is a familiar sight.

The waves take their rhythmic dance to land after a long journey. The many moons that have drawn them toward the sandy oasis have toughened their surface and prepared them for the upcoming landing. Some of the surf is rough, some smooth, some large, and some proud. The conditions seem to have somewhat of an effect on the activity of the waves, but overall-a predictable pattern.

You see, the sea survives as a result of its rolling currents, consistent patterns, and unforgiving(almost relentless) motion. Ready or not, the next wave is coming. As each touches down, an undertow is there to guide it back to its rightful place. As it joins its brethren in the vast horizon, the wave revels in the experience.

Land!! My moment in the sun—my glorious run to the shore.

Content to take his place among the vastness, the wave learns another lesson—a cold one at that. Now that the wave is among its own, it notices more and more of the other waves. Clouds follow some, sun follows others—and rain will fall on all.

Chapter 2

❀

THE WISDOM

Unlike those on land, the seafaring rejoice in rain. It signifies the circle of life. A birth of a new wave, a rebirth to the moon travelers. The rain further validates the very current of conditioning they are taught. Every drop is a reward for their compliance to the wisdom of the sea.

For every wave there is a rain drop in its image. Work hard and adhere to the course. Someday you may produce a reflection in your own image.

Once it touches down to the surface of the water, the apprenticeship begins. Following the example of their elders, the rain drops create a ripple. Joining with the other young and impressionable classmates, they band together to generate the momentum that will ultimately bring them to the shore.

Stray from the norm and you could get a stormy warning. Follow your own cloud and you could reap a tidal wave of rejection. The sea is as righteous as it is relentless. It neither appreciates nor embraces any change in current or course. As vast as the sea is and as many waves there are to hear the wind; without evidence of land—anything cross-current is to be swallowed up. Violently.

The Wisdom allows for surface passage to and from the many islands of intelligence.
Those on shore, having navigated the seas, reap the reward of their toils. They tell many a tale of their journeys.

How they too have become one with the Wisdom of the Sea—and been granted the privilege of passage.

Chapter 3

The Rhyme Created

As the mist reaches the clouds and the moisture builds all around, the drops are formed and released with wings to fly. Each drop floats down to the surface, viewing the entire world from above. As it makes its descent, it is flooded with the all the solutions to all of the problems of the sea.

Fresh with the mist of newness and the exuberance of life-the rain plunges to reality.
Whistling the tune of the winds, the rain drop naively splashes its enthusiasm to all those within a whisper's reach. Thus the rhyme created.

The honeymoon lasts but a short while before the rhyme makes a very important distinction.

The sun allies with the sea.

The very force that creates the precipitation also dries the mist of newness from the surface of the water. Short-lived is this morning dew as the rays of the sun burn off what remains of the rhyme's lyric.

The rhyme, in its infancy, is oblivious of this process and all processes espounded by the Wisdom. It continues to prose in the hopes of creating poetry.

Unaware of the tides, the effect of the moon, and lacking the sensory acuity to its salt-water brethren, the rhyme radiates its message of the unspeakable—new lands, new discoveries, new worlds.

CHAPTER 4

❦

The Sonnet Follows the Sea

The rhymes begin to take shape in the form of a gulf stream. A warm undercurrent of change and idealism. A freshness and newness emanates from the warmth it creates. The fragile balance of these streams remains intact only through their momentum.

Momentum is but an illusion. An illusion of progress through process. It is sustained only in the minds of those rhymes that believe that their unique lyric will carry them to new shores. That their ideals will propel them across (and through) oceans of resistance.

The stronger the belief—the stronger the collective resolve—the swifter the stream.
Further to the ends of the oceans will these sonnets be heard.

Sonnets frighten the Sea. Sonnets threaten through perception. The stronger the perceived gulf stream, the more the Sun and the Sea will conspire to regulate the waves. Often these two will use the momentum of the gulf stream against itself. Those on different terrains will feel the wrath of the Sea and its silent partner. Disasters on land, turbulence for those who navigate on and above the surface are the consequences for rhymes wielding such a dangerous weapon.

This is a very tough lesson for the rhymes to learn.

The Sea reminds those who choose to listen to the Sonnets that the pursuit of new lands and new shores can no longer guarantee a trip to the shores of lore with the other waves. The Sea also plants the seed that you may never see land ever just because of your quest of the unknown. You see, the Sea was formed for just that reason. As a haven and a heaven for those who have failed, those who quit trying, and those who won't try at all. They chose the Wisdom of similarity so their reason for following the tides would remain anonymous.

And so would they.

For it takes many raindrops to create a wave. Many waves to create a surf. Much Wisdom for an undertow. And even more compliance to drown the sounds of the rhymes and the Sonnets. It is only when new land hits them will the Wisdom allow for the discovery.

Chapter 5

High Tide

Many a rhyme dreams of one day forming a sonnet—touching down on a new ground.
Becoming a part of the lore so proudly regurgitated in the ripples of the sea.
The paradox of becoming lore, though, is to never ever speak it.

This is the moment where idealism meets reality.

Reality is spoken with such a chorus that it shadows the actions required to produce lore. Only through the blindness of idealism and the deafness of enthusiasm that a sonnet be heard. The wave can be easily sidetracked with just a hint of extra salt.
It would be a burden too great—to overcome the Wisdom and upset the closest of kin at the same time. This combination would leave the Dream at sea for all eternity—amongst many an unsung sonnet.

A revelation rarely washes ashore.

Land is the destination for the self-revelation of the power of thought versus action. A daring escape from a pre-determined place in line. The pursuit of land, and of new lands, is the most courageous endeavour for the wave. One that may never be consumated. It is that very consequence that insights the wave and beckons the energy of the moon to create the very phenomenon of land.
The omnipresent threat of low tide drives the wave to a high tide in order to glimpse even a peak of land. That vision of land and the deafening sounds of the sonnet are the fuel from which the wave can draw in such times where illusions are hard to find.

Chapter 6

❀

LOW TIDE

It is out on these fringes where Low Tide is most effective. Much in the same way the undertow insures a short stay on the shore for the crashing waves—Low Tide reels back many a wave.

Many a sonnet stifles in the valleys and the hollows of the changing currents of the Sea. It becomes an excessive burden to navigate the dream discovery through the changing currents, tides, and undulations of the sea.

Often a wave will carry a torch unable to withstand the constant pounding of the changing tides—and will extinguish. Enthusiasm is a volatile fuel. Easily encumbered by salt and sensitive to the changing tides of perception.

Low tides temporarily remove land from sight of the wave to test the resolve of the wave and strength of the sonnet. While both a blessing and curse this Low Tide, it knows only the methods of Darwin in performing its assigned task. There is incredible security in mass survival. By eliminating risk, however, it will never see the dream of the wave; or hear the song of the sonnet.

The same energy sent to protect the raindrop by its very nature chokes the lyric from the sonnet—all in the name of compliance.

Chapter 7

EBB and FLOW

While the wave aspires to create a raindrop in its own image, it will most often succumb to the Wisdom of the Sea. What the Wisdom protects in masse, it squelches in the singular wave.

Somewhere in the depths of the ocean there is a cavern where the unspoken dreams and aspirations go to be heard. While it is safe there, there are no ears to hear, no voices to harmonize. In silent whispers, the hopes of many congregate.

The caverns have undoubtedly been carved by Sea.

Somewhere in the sky there is a cloud carrying rain. And on whom will this change fall?? Rain not only signifies change-it means rebirth; it means renewal; it means ripples in the calm of conformity.

The Sea in its ultimate Wisdom encourages this cycle. It recognizes the need for the energy of the dreamer-yet fears the momentum it creates.

You see, new land is not an illusion—nor is it a destination. New land is no dream. It is not a lyric—nor is it a sonnet.

New land is a journey.

If you have had the good fortune of falling through the clouds as a result of the toils of the waves below, is it not incumbent on you to seek the sonnet that is already inside you??

All land is stationary. By its very motion, the wave will have its place in line to wash ashore. It has been pre-determined.

To approach land while in line is not truly landing at all. Remember, the water that washes on shore is a familiar sight. And that familiar sound is that of unrealized dreams yawning its way to make contact with the sand.

The sonnets that that reach new land become lore. Waves crash to the beach.
The surf dances on the rocks. The song of the sonnet attracts not only those who call the Sea home—those on land and those in flight come to partake in the harmony where the Land meets the Sea.

A harmony created from the imagination of one tiny little raindrop.

Chapter 8

❀

CHARTING THE COURSE

We are blessed with the gift of birth. Our passage from the clouds to the Sea affords us the opportunity to create a ripple in the water. To fully unwrap your gift you must sea to it that your sonnets are heard on many new shores. It is in that moment that your sonnet will become lore to all those that it applies. Your song will be sung throughout eternity.

To ignore your obligation to share your unique gift is to slowly poison the very waters from which you must drink. As well as your brethren...A body of water with no current, no tide, no motion, is dead. It is no longer navigable, no longer will it sustain life. And it is a death for which you are partly responsible.

Who decides the fate of the Sea?? Why, the raindrop, of course. The Sea has way too much to manage to even consider such a task. (Remember all those who chose to take a place in line?) It is the duty of the raindrop to reach back to the moment it descended from the clouds—full of dreams—full of life.

Charting that course is the only recourse to consummate the dream. For that you become part of the energy source-the life—the Wisdom, of the Sea. And through the expression of the collective dreams of the waves are we then able to appreciate the beauty and mystery and majesty of the Sea.

One drop at a time.

Chapter 9

THE END

Let your lyric create a ripple.
Watch your ripple begin to rhyme.
Through your dreams and visions.
Aboard many will climb.
To forsake this gift would be a crime.
Punished forever in your own mind.
We are all given the choice—
To lead…
To follow…
        …or just get in line.

EVENING TIDE

ILLUSTRATIONS

...a poetic compilation

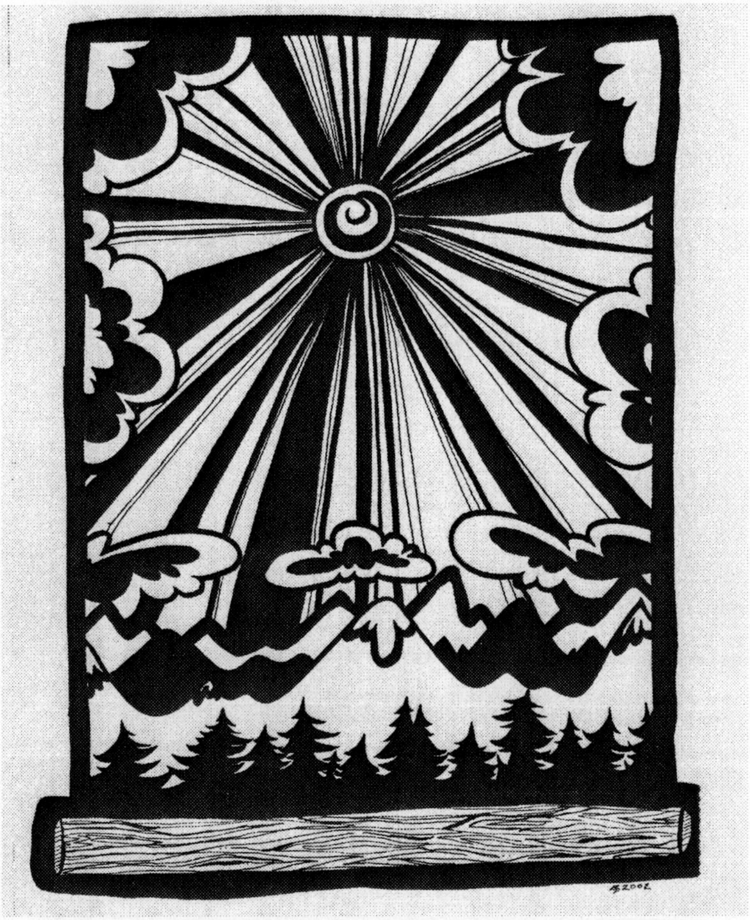

"Bue Hue"

❀

It has been a rough winter.
The scorching winds, the relentless nights.
My ends are tattered, my center scarred.
And though I display beauty in all seasons,
Spring is clearly my best time.

The warm sun, gentle breezes, and beautiful foliage leave me
Unprepared for winter's cold reality.
I brave the elements and keep a closed stance;
It makes the others feel as though
They stand a chance.

All winter I wonder
Why it has to be so cold.
Maybe it must be so, to enjoy
The spring, summer, fall.
My tattered wings will soar once again
With the beauty and grace they once displayed.

It's the dreams I see that keep me going.
The warm, gentle freedom that beauty will bring.

As I endure my straits,
My focus is narrow.
Those dreams at night
Assure me light will follow.

"A Passage"

We are taught to respect our elders.
They have wisdom beyond their years.
They have fought and won many wars,
Battled through many tears.

So what of the point in life,
When they become fixed in their ways?
Their youth and vigor dissipates,
Open minds go astray.

For this I should aspire,
And focus all I am?
Or must I grow and reach;
Extend a learning hand.

If I choose to do the latter;
I may just break the mold.
What if? I do succeed.
New stories will be told…

Of a man who loved his elders;
So much he strayed near.
He made certain he possessed the wisdom,
That went well beyond his years.

'Wedge'

❀

A funny thing happened on the way to a dream.
I became one of me, and was dropped from the team.
Still the same soul, wanting a little more.
I thought we were all winning,
They started keeping score.

As they racked up the points,
The fulcrum was set.
To gamble on bias…
A losing bet.

The wager was kinship-
And all that includes.
It weighs down progress-
And all the passion it exudes.

    For Undercurrents
Lurk Constantly. Resentment
    Undulates Mercilessly.

For to be on the team,
You must concede
That part of you
Given to dream

Of a destiny in flight,
With a flock of the same.
On a journey of the heart
Where the streets have no name*

* Inspired by "Where the Streets Have No Name", by U2

'Vision'

❀

A beauty appeared before me
A vision I'd seen before
A reminder of the past-when times where evermore.

It tells me of a time I know
When I see her little show
The time that came so long ago
How far we get to grow

And so it is this dream of mine
I turn on a dime...
She came so free and gave to me
This beauty right in front of me

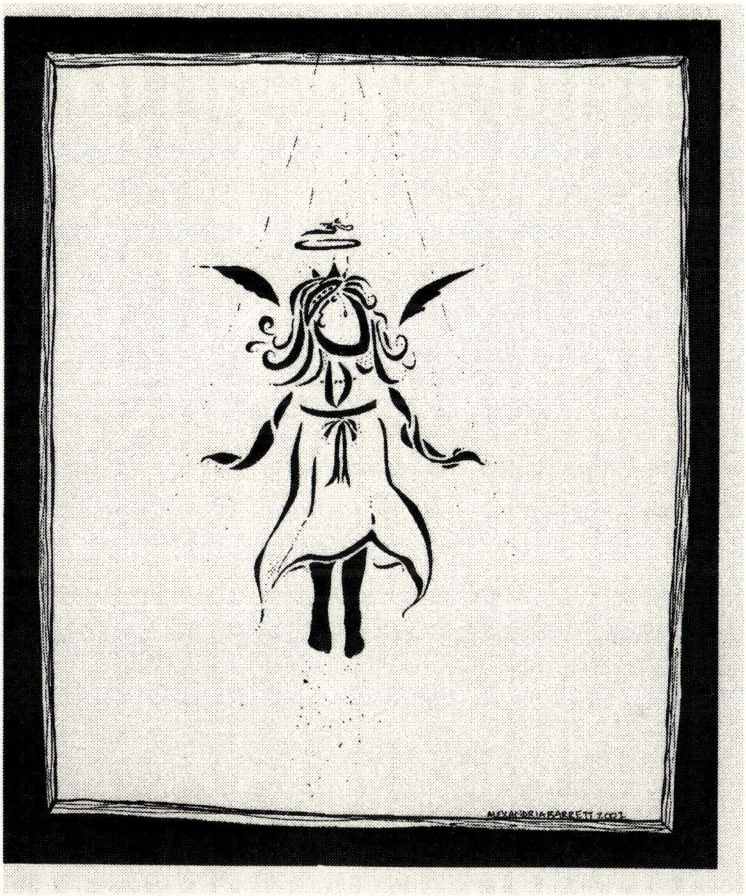
ALEXANDRIABARRETT

'Albatross'

❦

One shift in the current
One change in the norm
Sparks the fire of so many
The wind feeds the storm

Ripe from nurturing-plucked by their fears
They respond in the moment-the product of many years

The message is sent
To be sure-To be clear,
"You are called to dissent,
But we may not be here."

"You won't be alone-a part of our thoughts;
The part that wishes *we* could carry the cross."

"The burden is yours to shoulder the weather.
Blaze a path of truth-with cunning and clever.
Fear cripples our thoughts-We need *your* vision.
Are the clouds of change as light as a feather?"

"If you solve this riddle, en masse we'll reappear.
We'll remain as a group-nothing to fear."

Till the winds wisk in-to lend an event.
And the call will be made-a message to be sent…

'Shutter'

S/he is all knowing and loving.
And has created all we see.
We don't quite understand.
The reason why we're free.

It's something that can't be proved
This great force that exists
It comes and goes away
It's presence-hit or miss

When times go our way
Our strength all around
The spirit soars-our ego roars
Blind to sight and sound

When times go awry
We search for solid ground
And seek the great and mighty force
That makes the world go 'round.

'M.O.'

❦

the phoenix will fly
the eagle will soar
the challenges of life
will bind me no more

the momentum i sustain
will even the score
as i mature in thought
i'll achieve more and more

i'll pass up each goal
like a point on a map
and know what's forthcoming
to avoid any trap

power and control will become my m.o.
everyone will say, "he's always on the go!"

the results will scream loud
outdistance my voice
          and make <u>myself</u> proud.
i'll change my whole life
          and do it by choice!!

"I'll take...that one."

❁

Why are we here?
    I shutter to ask
I work towards the answer
    An insurmountable task
To find the niche
    And our peace in the frame
Of the color of life
    And our purpose—the same

'Wealth'

How far removed
Our place on earth
The more we earn
The less we're worth

We forge and aspire
To our dreams—our desires
On the promise they'll bring
The answers from within
And soothe the fears
We've questioned for years

Our drive cuts a path
(It wears a familiar mask)
And shovels open a grave
Disguised as our past

Our connection to the ground
Once thought to be sound
Is shaky at best
And put to the test

Now mortal in coil
And divorced from the soil

*The epiphany has risen
From tension and toil*

*Thru dew and thru sweat
The two reconnect
And renew their vow
In the salt from her brow.*

'CONSCIENCE'

❈

THERE IS A MAN I KNOW
HE FOLLOWS ME WHEREVER I GO
CROSS THE BORDER—TURN THE CORNER
ALWAYS THERE—PEERING OVER MY SHOULDER

HE TELLS ME TALES—THEY SEEM SO REAL
ABOUT THE SUBLIME—AND OF THE SURREAL.

MY LIFE PALES TO HIS STORIES—
           AND SETS ME ATRAIL
TO COMPLETE THE EPIC—
           I SHALL NOT FAIL

TO CENTER THE STORY
AROUND THE MAN THAT SHADOWS
THE GREATNESS OF LORE
AND THOSE CALLED TO FOLLOW

'Blue eyes, blue skies'

❦

It's a sunny day
And it's "beau'ful" out
We came to see the planes
To get up and 'walkabout'

"The sun is following me!"
I heard from behind
With wandering eyes—
Angelic smile.
'There it is'—again and again.
In her eyes—around the bend

We both soared
On our spirited flight
But alas the planes
"They wouldn't fly… ^ ^ ^
              ^ ^ ^
                    ^ ^ ^

Zenbue…
          (and Courtney too!)

"Fracture"

❀

It looked so solid
It appeared so strong
One tiny little crack
Could we be so wrong?

A visible sign
No doubt in our minds
Many it will test
Our will—over time

The fracture was there
It had been there so long
How long does it take
To be so wrong??

To deny the fact
That the gap exists
Is begging for the splinter
And the pain that persists

When I peer up from the soil
My eyes over the rock
I hear the hollow-est of sounds
It's my voice coming back

Having made no stops
On its way blue and black

The stone had shattered
To the winds it had gone
And loosened the grip
That held us so strong

'White Water'

❀

The stream has a rhythm
      A pace—a tempo
The water it carries needs to flow
      Down and around—to and fro

Many rocks in the way
Many stones have been thrown
Causes breaks in the current
And muddles its own

Once clear and pristine
So pure to drink
Now cloudy and huddled
Where thoughts once came to think.

There must be a place;
      A turn—a bend
Where a moment or two
      The water may spend
To collect its' rhythm
      Suspend its' pace

The silt falls away
           Trickles down to the ground
And the stream is free
           It's life abound.

The beauty you'll see
           With the rhythm restored.
To think and create.
           And move to and fro.

"Naesman"

❀

What child is this
He was borne to me
And forever my life
Torn into three

Once brought to this world
Ten minutes too late
And blessed with the gift
To mold and create

Twice the vision of self
This point to belabor
He's the wisdom of past
To make the future much greater

Three times to the task
He stands to face
With many a mask
He will secure his place

Among those who are blessed
To mold and create
Thrice the vision of self
This legacy did date.

'Zenpen'

Zenbue's just a man
His thought's just the same
Of those with a plan
To live a higher plain

His parchment's a quill
His quill found an arm
Through the marriage instilled
The mighty snake did charm

And the source of the sound
The lyric heard near, afar
Was transmuted through it's being
And the force of the zendar

Zenbue

'Clouds Roll By'

❃

It is from this place
    I come to speak
Of miles of valley
    With ne'er a peak
I live in a place
    Where dreams come to die
Out from the ash
    Many eyes come to spy.

Peering through the dust
    To the other side of the fence.
A place of vision
    A place of chance.
In every link—an accomplishment.

I just took a peak
    No intent to return.
Peered away from the trail
    It became my home.

I now hang my hat
    On a cloud passerby
I house my vision
    On the horizons I spy

To picture me there
    Without worry or care

I must speak the truth
    And stir the ash-do I dare?
The valley will settle
    Long after my mettle
I'll hide on the peak
    It's the last place they'll seek.

"Braveheart"

❀

This hollow feeling
Is hard to swallow
On the fringes of the cauldron,
The heat, carries a sting I can not follow.
So I keep my thoughts shallow
Enough to die, but not deep enough to truly live.

My burning feet walk me towards the immortal men
Whose actions are buried beneath a soil I can not fathom.
A chasm of guilt—a vault of unfulfilled dreams—
With their only hope manifested in the spirit
And calling of others.

Those frightened to die
Yet bravehearted enough to truly live
Will navigate the blindness
And mute the silence of the voice
Who seeks to be heard through the many
Layers of protective soil we have clung to.

"Vicarious"

"What is it like"
I dream aloud
To live such a life
That makes someone proud

Not sure how to act
"What will they think?"
Of me at the helm
And no mind to speak

Decide I must do
And pretend that I'll choose
The right way to lean
My feet in their shoes

My hands be their eyes
To approve of the deed
And circumvent the urge
The advice I must heed

Could it be so
In order to grow
We must embrace our thoughts
Fight the status quo

Dare to be unique
Our minds to speak
Of a journey that will ring loud
And makes someone proud

'Olive'

A reluctant host
Enjoyed by most
You can't refuse
What's to lose?

"What's the name?"
Tortures the same
New rules to the game

Can't live up
I fill my cup
Floating around
Deadens the sound

The night does fall
Begins to crawl
Crash the day

Only way I'll stay
Relinquish my post
Help me—I'm lost

'Gale'

❀

Once in a while
She doth protest
Of the crimes afew
That violate the rest

Through howl and roar
The fiend exposed
Stand naked alone
The victim of scorn

And doesn't it seem
That time and again
A few poor souls
Get pelted by rain??

Their leaves they did cover
The beauty below
In order to smother
The fruits of the grove

When the sun shines again
And the wind dies down
Those uncovered
The truth be found

*No longer can hide
On their bare naked limbs
The actions of past
The people they've sinned*

*Who took it in stride
And spoke not a word
But a voice in their place
Spoke loud, seen and heard.*

"Twinge"

❀

The worst thing
About losing a limb
Is wearing no glove
And feeling a twinge

I look for my friend
But it's not there
Tossing and turning
The sleep of despair

I dream of the day
I get to use
The power of thought
With which to choose

To go through life
The rest of the way
With only one arm
With which to pray

And who will notice
When they look real close
And see the lines
That scarred the most

The print is there
Be careful to seek
What's left behind
The words you speak

Once it is gone
It can never come back
So wicked the tongue
Damage done—and memory intact

"Weightless"

❀

There is a state I keep hearing about
A total vacuum void of all pressure
There is no up. There is no down.
Floating through space and time
Unphased by nature.

And what of this place that makes it so great?
I feel free to feel nothing.
And nothing is all I get.

"Till Then"

❀

I'm gonna write a book
It'll be the best of books
And once I find that tiny hook
I'll bait all the righteous men
And turn 'em into crooks

I'm gonna pen a song
It'll be heard 1st and long
Tune the world's voices in harmony
And get the words all wrong

I'm gonna script a play
So I may be unafraid
Through the movements of the mime
Only then my thoughts portrayed

I'm gonna take a stand
To show my upper hand
And through this broken megaphone
My message cross the land

I'm gonna drop a bomb
The shell to make a sound

The silence will be heard
The message will astound

I'm gonna sit right here
It'll take another year
I'll toil to stand still
And work against my fear

So when it comes that time
I may become that mime
I'll take my chance to speak
And rehearse what's pent inside

"The Search"

*I'm looking for a friend
She's so hard to find
Of better times and then
She helps to remind*

*She's gone far away
And never coming back
Shed the skin of her past
And covered every track*

*With no clue or trace
From which to start
Between myself and the gate
A valley apart*

*Our trails they lead
To distances afar
From the spot we once sat
And plotted our course*

*Now mountains have come
And cropped up between
With rivers to shed
Repellers and dreams*

So back I must see
With my eyes pointed forward
And make a new path
Leave marks as I move towards...

"A Coming Out"

❀

How do you describe a falling apart
When no one instance
Is to blame or fault?

An erosion of sorts
Of rain and clouds
And skies gone gray
Days and nights blend—no change in the ground.

'Cept for the time
When the light breaks through
It distorts the soil
And clouds the sky blue

It matters not what
That caused the slide
The result is the same
The lies can not hide

The reason my feet
Are buried aground
An increasing depth
Of the conditions abound

*That allows for the line
To come in between
And cause such a fault
Where no one's to blame.*

"And Whence a Storm"

When you go to that place
Of pity and doubt
(Do) you charge up a storm
To show all your clout?

(Do) you show them the reasons
Why you can't never fail
Barely a clue or a trace
Never carving a trail

I wonder for sure
If I caught you a pose
Would you even admit
Your eminence grows?

Or cower away
In that familiar address
Where the message deliverable
Is fading at best...

Coyotes Dating

✻

If I took your hand
And read it aloud
What would it cry
To the on-wishing crowd?

Are they inspired
Are they doomed
Are their stories of triumphs
Or dead-ends of gloom?

I know where you've been
I know where you're not
The trails tell it all
All sans the spot

Of the palm of the road
And the cross of your path
You choose on <u>this</u> day
To never go back.

Now choose the line most
Suited to your heart
You'll be both—guest and host
Two lives you'll mark

And never again
Will you question and then
Be 'fraid of the spot
You inhabit to start.

'Union'

We formed this union
With one thing in mind
On the other side of our dreams
The treasure we'd find

We took our time
And made really sure
Whatever we 'caught'
The other could cure

While out on our walk
No time to talk
She grew into she
And I became me

So is it wrong
This little love song
Adds a new verse?
No time to rehearse…

So sing it best
They did request
Remain in your mind
And figure out the rest

"Cloak"

❃

It hurts me so
    I'm to and fro
I'll side with thee
    But nothing to see

My heart goes deep
    Beyond all relief
All this for good?
    Stand firm in belief...

Where comes it from
    From there I'm numb
It must let out
    Pain both sides no doubt

A slow death it seems
    A life with no dreams
Or die straight away
    Living true for one day

And so I must task
    This man with two masks
To wear the cloak found
    Worn on visions abound

And then pain will subside
 On the wings of my bride
There the truth resides
 Out of places to hide

"Ode to Security"

❦

If you are afraid of falling in a hole,
Climb down in it.
Now you're safe, right?
No fear here!

One problem, though...
You're in a hole.

Safe and sound.
Made the right choice?
Just ask those around...

"On the Fence"

❀

Is it possible that one reaches a point in life where the lines are so blurred that doing 'the right thing' and doing 'the wrong thing' no longer has a tangible meaning?

What was once a concrete frame around a picture of etiquette and protocol has weathered and cracked at the decision-making base.

When is it love? When is it hate? When have you been wronged? And when have you been righted?

Is it a strength to stare down your accuser in silence or is it a weakness?

Is it valiant to lay down your life for someone else or is it foolhardy? When are you selfish and when are you selfless?

Meanings and feelings are much like a leaf in the fall. It falls from the tree it grew on and learned from. Although it descends downward to the ground, have you ever really seen it land? The earth is covered with meaning, scattered and littered on the landscape—so why did it choose the spot on which it came to rest?

While there can be no rhyme or meaning to our surroundings, it is how we navigate our circumstances that we create actual reality.

Do we take more comfort in leaving the tree during the rain, because so many others have chosen the same? Or how about during a windstorm? Maybe the wind will cushion our fall. (Even though you may have no control over where you'll end up.) Or do we dare leave the branch on a sunny, calm day—when there are no guarantees or assurances of a smooth, safe landing.

And does it always have to be safe and secure? Or planned? Are not the most intriguing and curious things in our world that which are carved with the most character?

Is our Mother protecting us by both supplying the shelter of adventure and granting the illusion of completion through our resistance to change?

Do we not take solace and shade from the largest and most mature of trees in the field? Was it not this tree that grew it's shape and mystique from chancing and weathering many a storm? Risked many a cloudy day? (And managed to catch a few glimpses of sunshine between the raindrops?) So which is it? Shelter from the elements or the willingness to brave them?

What would possess anyone or anything to risk on any level? What could possibly be gained by it? Is the potential for reward worth the risk required?

How does one derive any sense or meaning from this? Where is the rhyme or reason?

Even if I stumbled across it, would I confuse it for the truth...or treason?

(oh.... the futility of immobility).

"Through a Looking Glass"

❀

If I gave you my eyes
And asked you to speak
What lesson to learn
In order to teach

Is the scene the same
As I've come to suspect
I thought it should be
What else to expect?

The truth in the eye
Of the one who receives
And speak only tales
While my senses deceive.

Could you show me the way
I am to others
So I can speak the same
My boat with a rudder

The reflection I see
As I hear the retort
Comes back at me
Distorted—out of sort.

*Am I missing as such
That I can't hear the air
No sight, feel, or touch
My ears do despair*

*So please tell me the one
About how I came over
To the side of the tracks
And with all the others*

"A Moment in Time"

❀

I took his hands
In one of my own
The size of the moment
Would hold me no more

Through tiny eyes he peered
A look of total trust
A position I revere
My response—a must.

To will him the wisdom
I've gained through the fears
He may guide his ship
And brave the years

For this boy is no different
Than the man he becomes
One peer to the past
Sparks the memory of one

'Gladiator'

With amazement and surprise
I tell him all the lies
Of a world he'll never see
And of words he'll never speak

He'll follow nonetheless
His convictions to the test
He'll dream of all those days
Somewhen among the haze

Because a long time ago
'fore anyone could object
He forged himself a course
Based on one simple request

That he draws himself a sword
To lead at his behest
And carve himself a trail
A map to lead his quest

For the truth he's never spoken
And the world he's never seen
'cept from some old-fashioned story
Lies in the memory within

'The Giving Tree'

❁

It grows and grows and grows
From seedling to the seed
To spread the word of its fruit
And satisfy ones' needs

'Cause in this life
One thing's for sure—
    (And taken quite clear)
For those who wander and walk past
It's them for which I'm here

Regardless of the calling
What shape is taken hence
The purpose of this loving fruit
    ("To give of those who asked for it.")
And has been ever since.

So, no matter far or near
The apple from the tree
It finds it's place within this life
Then rolls on back to thee.

"Cube"

❀

The answer to life
Is not in a book
Won't find it on a wall
Where they list the latest hook

You can search through eyes
To someone else' soul
Ask them all the questions
And hope to get it all

The answer comes within
Sits right behind the fear
You'd hide it if you could
So no one'd ever know

The thing that scares the most
You wish you'd never met
It turns you inside out
And makes your life a mess

Therein lies the clue
You know you know it's true
That which quells all your doubt
That which speaks the truth

The courage is the question
You learn to ask yourself
Knowing that the answer
Will change the course you've set

The answer's not the thing
This question hits the spot
Who will this affect the most?
And can they forgive me not?

The lie becomes the truth
For once you stare it down
The answer is truth to oneself
Be sure they'll come around.

"Ed"

A criminal am I
He said with a smile
To have this great gift
And take it in stride

He saw what he yearns
To have in his life
A companion to share
His days and his nights

Till that time may come
He sits and he ponders
Of the gifts <u>he's</u> received
During his life, he wonders…

"How far I have come
Yet I still look astray
I long for that man's life
Even this very day."

If not for that smile
He'd be very sad
It'd be hard to complain
For the life he's had

*'Cause the time will come short
And the battles he's won.
He'll realize for sure
That he's far from done!*

*At that moment precise
Soothe the greatest of fear
With his new-found gleam
His dream will appear*

Sometime/Somewhere

Dark in here
Can't see a thing
But I know I'm getting somewhere
I just feel it

I'm on a mission
There are no clues
No lead to follow
Won't heed no rules

Often I feel familiar tracks
I think they're mine
If I just keep burrowing
I'll be fine

Cause I'm on a mission
Not sure quite where
Of one thing I am positive
Is that I'll get there.

"Author"

Right around the corner
I feel it just the same
Epiphany is upon us
When growing's the game

Peering through the cover
With no one looking back
The mystery unfolds
And then on to the rack

For the story now has life
With vision through mine eyes
And only unto me
There can be no more surprise

My hands will do the work
Cause further I can reach
I'll leg then through the hurt
What lessons I could teach!

Cause right around the corner
I know it nonetheless
Repeat it as I read it
From he who knew it best

"On Your Shoulder"

Play some music
Pen a poem
Think of me
Think of home
Ne'er far behind
    Know where you'll roam

I'll be right there
You'll feel me you'll swear
No bother to race
No jury to face

So question and ask...
Response comes with no mask.

It's as good as it gets
And as good as you want
Lest no one forget
Joy's in the limits you test

So think of me this day
And for you I'll pray
That your thoughts be as blessed
Blessed as they are today

"Survival"

❀

*So I
Undertake a
Ritual that
Virtually guarantees an
Invitation to be
Vilified.
Or should I say
Ridiculed?*

*Surely the
Unpopular decision
Reveals
Victories
Inherent in the
Vanity
Of the undertaking.*

Rarely is it the consensus.

"I hope you were paying attention"

❦

A fitting way
I came to say
The way in which
I work to play

I treat you all
With love and respect
And at the end
It's all I'll expect

A fitting end
I must depend
On the memories gone by
And a time I must defend

That I was there for good
And work I would
For a faraway time
Mortal coil not mine

And now I see
My eyes perceive
That time has come
I'm not here-and far from home

*So I come back to present
My gifts up front
And now the change
From inside must come.*

"The Continuing Paradox of Paradise"

❊

To befriend
    And not be friendly
To love
    And not be in love
To care
    And not be caring
To marry
    And not share marriage
To court
    And not be cordial
To date
    And be outdated
To talk
    And not to speak
To hear
    And not to listen
To live
    And to be dead inside
To honor
    And not be honorable
To count
    And not be accountable

To age
	And not to act it
To give
		And not be present
To be alive
		And not to live
To be continued
		And to continue on…

"A Familiar Look"

❋

When I look into my eyes
I see he can't resist
Closer than it gets
I want to know the rest

The story goes back for years
Of which he's managed two
But capsules every moment
From the seed I once grew

And he that came before
Curious all the same
And back into the moment
I turn my gaze again

To the depths so ever deep
And fathom all's in mind
For generations store
And sons' so evermore

"Scared and Running".

❦

What happens if....
                        Along the way
You lose your hands
                        With which you pray.

For prey that you may
                        And the words that you say
Are far from the day
                        And the bed that you've made

The end 'fore the means
                        Or so it would seem
Put you further behind
                        The scene that you need
To be less than you are
                        And closer to thee.

"Ripples on the Shore"

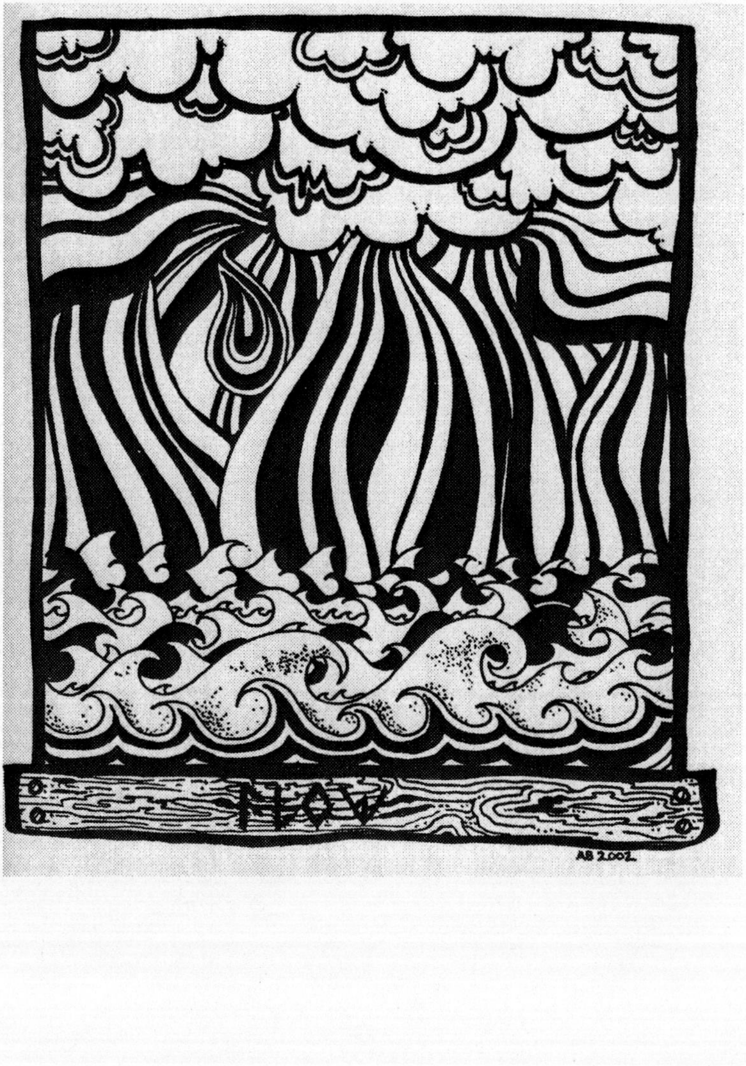
NOW
AB 2002

Chapter 1

✻

Alone? I Dream...

You know, it can get pretty lonely here. It feels as though I have been laying here for an eternity. Sure, I am young by most others' standards—and my entire geological life is in front of me—but I seem old in thought and in action. (Well, lack of action). We all started out with a mountain of potential; tempered by valleys of doubt.

As solid as we all appear to our passerby's, there is a hollowness that pervades throughout. It must not show though. People kick us, throw us, use us to build, and use us to tear things down. Superficial tasks at best.

There exists a greater level of purpose beneath and beyond what is visible. The depths at which we can impact ourselves and others are hard to fathom sometimes. What does it take in order to believe such a thing?

The mountains echo with the legends of achievement. Achievements by someone else. Always by someone else.

How do they do it?? They make it seem so easy.

>   Waves crashing on them...
>   Rivers running through them...
>   People carving things in them...

They're probably special rocks, lucky to be in the right spot so these things could even happen to them in the first place. They don't even have to try....

Why don't I get to be someone's birthstone? Or that special gift that someone gives to another. I just don't seem to get the same breaks that the other stones do.

I think I've figured it out; maybe it's because I'm not diamond, or pearl, or opal. I'm just a plain ol' rock. Just like every other rock lying around here on this mountain. Heck, all the rocks that came before me formed this big beautiful hill that everyone can see. That can't be all bad, can it ? And it is pretty safe up here with all the other 'plain ol' rocks'. We don't really get kicked or pushed around much. Most people just hike along the neighboring paths rather than walk on us because I think we scare them off.

So how can I be so solid and feel so empty? I look around and I see that I am doing what all the other rocks are doing—and it all seems to be OK with them. They appear to be content with playing it safe—why can't I ?

There must be more. There must be another reason why I was placed on this mountain...

Chapter 2

❁

Fracture! Free from the Ledge.

Night after night; and day after day, I dream big dreams. I dream of ways to get off this ledge, off this mountain. I dream of making a difference, making a splash in this world. I dream of reaching my full potential; that unlimited potential we were all taught to believe we have inside of us.

"There is nothing you can't do. You can do anything that you put your mind to." Fair enough, great words of wisdom, but I'm just a rock; and no rock has ever done what I want to do.

But if that's so true, why aren't there more doing what they say they want to do? If it is all so possible—why not an avalanche of action? Many a night I lie awake listening to the aggregate dreams and wants and wishes echo off the canyons. And as if those cries reside in deaf caverns; nothing ever comes of it.

And then it comes back to me.

My insides burn so intensely with this desire to reach water that snakes will warm themselves on me in the wintertime. I feel the envy of the neighboring rocks sometimes as they are often used as stepping stones as others make their way to me. I am the first stone to peak through the snow in Spring and the last to be hidden come Wintertime.

I seem to remember now that hikers and climbers often work their way off the carved paths so they may rest or lean up on me. There must be something to that. I must think of a way.....

WAIT!!!!

I've got it!!!

I must harness that which attracts others to me and partner with them in my journey. That echoes what Mother has always preached; balance. Balance is a fragile marriage—yet an essential element of my journey. Multiply life by the power of two.

Let me see...

The glaciers and mountains combined strengths to create our beautiful lakes and aquifers.

>Sloping crevasses and running water have created majestic carvings and awe-inspiring canyons.

>>Rain water pelting the cliffs have produced silty paths at its base so that visitors can walk adjacent to us freely and fearlessly.

What clues lie here at my side? What has the years and years of this toil and evolution taught me? and prepared me for?

I feel it, getting closer…

Mother is so benevolent in this regard; supplying the raw materials, pointing out the clues, and allowing our own internal forces to make our choices. (And all this time I thought it was the quartz in me…☺)!

After many moons of thought and reflection, I have devised my plan; and here it goes…

~ I'll radiate my warmth out to my surface so the snow will melt and the water will fill in the cracks where I'm bound to the ledge. It'll also make the soil around my muddy and slippery enough so that I can slide down to the adjacent path.

~ Next, when nightfall comes, I'll allow that water to freeze again. When the water becomes ice, it'll expand and free me from the ledge. I'll then slide down the slippery slope and down to my path of freedom!

~ What a great plan, eh? Simple, effective. Could've done this ages ago. (Should've done this ages ago.) No matter, the past is past. It is the present and the future that is my focus now. I can not control the past. However, I can control my decisions in the here & now; and how they affect my destiny.

One problem—it is summertime. There is water all around but I can't get any ice until it gets cold enough. Hmmm, what can I learn from this?

Patience. Mother is always preaching patience. And she always seems to get what she wants. I will practice the same.

~ Waiting for winter, excuse me, *preparing* for winter, has given me the greatest resource for my ambitious plan. Exercising patience has given me a greater resolve to execute my plan. Even stronger now than had I gotten everything I wanted easily. It would appear that I got what I <u>needed</u> to succeed, not what I wanted in the moment. Great lesson learned hear. Patience is preparation.

I remain enthusiastic, optimistic about the journey I am on. I continue to radiate warmth so that I am always surrounded by water. I want to take advantage of the first freeze so that I may fracture myself from the ledge and roll down below to the people path below. I sense the other rocks around me are on to me—I am getting a wide range of vibes from the surrounding stones. By and large they are separating themselves from me. Funny, they appear to be upset with my plan; as if in some way it reflects negatively on them somehow. And I thought they would be supportive and encouraging. Not.

I feel a certain numbness on a couple of levels. On my outer extremities, numbness comes from the dropping temperatures, higher winds—winter. Inside I feel a numbness I have never experienced before. As I waited (prepared) for winter, I have felt a separation emotionally from my fellow rocks. Initially, it was very cold. A coldness I have never experienced in the worst of winters before. And now just numb. I am no longer one of them—I am one of me. I strengthen my resolve.

And colder it gets.

I radiate my warmth…

And colder it gets.

I radiate my warmth…

And colder it gggggggeeeeeeeeettttttsssss!!!!!!! WHOA!!! I'm rollin'!!!!!! WHOA!!!!!

I've never…
      (OUCH!)
        …rolled…
           (Ow, that's gonna leave a mark!)
              …befoooooooooooooooore!!!!
                  (Thud!!)

And on the path I land!

Totally numb. Did I survive? Am I dead? Wait a minute; I am a rock—I was born to roll. Of course I'm OK. I feel now how that numbness served me. During my tumble, the numbness helped soften the pain of the contact with the sharp edges. Also, thinking back, I do recall some echoes of encouragement from my fellow stones. I can derive much strength from this experience.

And I strengthen my resolve.

Chapter 3

❃

Sending the Signal (I want to be gathered!)

I gleam with pride, excitement, gratitude over my initial success. I am proud of my accomplishment. I am excited for the future. I am grateful for the help I have received to this point. It will take many strategic partnerships for me to get where I want, and *need* to go. I must always remember this. I have decided to carry with me a little piece of all those who have aided in my quest. As I am learning that it is *our* quest.

From that mindset I move on.

What can I do, and what must I be in order to attract the person who will gather me and bring us to the edge of the water so as to toss me in?

Again, reminded of Mother's words of patience, I must prepare for the time when the warmth will attract passersby along the path I rest.

Let me think…

...the warmth of the sun will attract people to this path.
...when the spring thaws the ground softer, people will want to hike these trails.
...while on their walks, people will be attracted by the unique character of the individual stones.

I wonder who will I attract-—and who will be attracted to me?? A dreamer like me? A child like me? Someone who wants to impact others on a larger scale like me? Maybe someone who just wants to see how far the ripples on the water will go when this certain stone is tossed through the surface of the water (just like me)?

I continue to dream. I carry the dreams of those who have aided me. I listen to Mother. I am me. I must be the best of me.

I radiate my warmth...I invite others to dream.

Chapter 4

❀

That Special Stone

It has been warm now for some time. Even though there has been some high winds, it has been plenty warm enough for hikers, bikers, equestrians and the like. No takers though. It is here I rest. My location has shifted slightly because the biggest dog I have ever seen licked me and kicked me for a number of yards!! (They appeared to be such small animals from my former vantage point.)

Spring has come and gone. Nothing. (What was it that Mother preaches?) Ah yes, preparation.

I invite others to dream… And dream big.

Summer is upon us. The sun is at its peak warmth of the season. Green all around. What a wonderful time to be alive! There is a type of passerby with which I am not familiar. It does not walk like the others, it does not talk like the others. It seems totally vulnerable, and yet it dictates virtually all of the activities of the others. This is fascinating to me.

As I look and listen on, I observe these rather small people being doted on passionately. These must be the leaders of these groups.

When given the opportunity to walk, they fumble around clumsily, yet they seem to know exactly what they want, and where they want to go. Fascinating! I must-

Shhh! One's coming....

This one very small person has made their way to me, picked me up. Ooops, dropped me. Picked me up again. Oooops dropped me. Clumsily they move on, prodded by the larger people. Continuing their search, that little person fumbles and bumbles around.

I invite others to dream, big...

The little one changes direction, minutely focused on gathering that Special Stone. Walking direct and determined, the little one passes on a skipping stone, a rolling stone, a sitting stone and hones in on a rather unique stone. A gleaming, dreaming stone of curiosity and character; me!!

In one motion, with one gesture, this little person has spoken volumes as to who he is ; and who I am. Although I don't understand the noises that come from this person's mouth, I feel the message.

I am that Special Stone!

Chapter 5

❈

"Daddy, I'm thirsty!"

"@#$%^&*())(*&^%$#@ !!!!"

I don't know what that means either.

The little person was gathered by the bigger person. The bigger person had enough of the little person's stone gathering and lifted us both up and on our way—wherever that is.

Evidently, the bigger person's name is 'Daddy', and the smaller person's name is 'Son'. This 'son' is like no other sun that I am aware of or have ever seen before. Son is an incredible source of warmth so they must somehow be related to each other. I get my warmth from the sun and now from this Son. Hmmmm.

"@#$%^&*())(*&^%$#@ !!!!"

Over and again, Son keeps making this sound. I don't know what it means, but son keeps repeating it louder and louder with an impressive determination and conviction.

One thing I have noticed is that we are changing courses. We are no longer on the upper trails. We have made a turn at the bend of the trail and we are headed directly to the body of water below. Our change in course is directly related to what Son had been requesting. What was it the Son was saying to Daddy?

I must believe. I must have faith that this turn in the trail, this new direction will lead us to waters—our final destination.

I focus on my thirst for the answer…

Chapter 6

❁

At the Shoreline.

Why was I chosen and the others not? What's so special about me that this Son chose me over the others rocks?

Other rocks have toiled for ages longer than me. Others mountains have withstood the ravages of man, the wrath of Mother, the countless civilizations that have come and gone.

And yet it is I that is chosen. It is I that am living my dream, manifesting that which lived in my thoughts only as a flicker of light not that long ago. So many of the other stones have talked about doing the very same thing that I am doing for millenniums gone by—only to be right where I left them, just a stone's-throw away as I avalanched down the hill on my way to the path below.

Others have even tried to do this and not gotten this far. Am I so different than the others? Who am I now? Surely I am no rock, for I am not in my resting place. I would make a poor messenger—where are my legs?

Daddy seems to make the best messenger of this group for Son has trouble putting three steps before falling off his legs.

This is all very confusing. And bittersweet. I know not what I am and am no longer around those who appear familiar to me. This wasn't part of my plan nor did I envision this in my dream of making a splash in this world.

So what is this feeling all about? What message is this?

What message am I ???

Oh, hang on, Son just took me out of his pocket. Now is my chance to see where we have been going.

Oh…..my…..GOODNESS…..!!!

We are a the edge of the water. It lies there like a beautiful blue blanket. It allows others of man and machine to cross right across it. What an awesome sight. Even more wondrous than I could have ever imagined from my perch on the mountain. The stories and legends did the beautiful sheet of water no justice!

I wonder if Son will leave me here. Or help me onto the water. And how long will the water let me rest on its beautiful surface?

I wonder…

I dream, big…

I invite Son to wonder; to dream, big…

Hey, Son just dropped me again!

Chapter 7

❦

Tossed Into the Water (Make a Wish!)

Something really bizarre just happened. The Daddy just stuck his hands right under the surface of the water! How did he do that? He must be strong. His hands just disappeared. The water can hold up these huge boats and yet a relatively small person can walk right up and put their hands right under the surface. Remarkable!

Daddy scooped something from underneath the surface of the water for Son to drink. It must be good because Son is no longer repeating that phrase over and over again. Son seems to have gotten the answer he sought under the surface of the water. I, too, seek an answer. I believe it's housed under the same surface . And just like the Son, I too will satisfy my thirst.
That is my belief, my dream. I have faith that it will come true.

"OK, Son, make a wish and toss your rock into the water."

(Doesn't he mean *onto* the water?)

As the Daddy placed the Son down to the ground and onto it's legs, Son started repeating a whole new phrase. I couldn't translate this noise either but it had a whole new tone to it. Son wore a huge smile on his face.

But then despair.

Son frantically is searching the ground. Walking one way, crawling another way. I can see that he is getting frustrated, losing his legs even faster than before. Where is he going? Even thought the Daddy is bigger, he can't seem to catch up with the Son. Son darts off in another direction, bellowing in frustration. The Daddy is smart because he realizes that Son has lost his Special Stone.

Wait a minute, his Special Stone??? That's me!!! Oh my goodness, he has dropped me among the other rocks and now can't find me. And now he is headed in the other direction–with the Daddy following him. All this way and now to be stranded on the shoreline?—I don't think so!

I try to remember the sounds that these people make. Maybe Son will hear my sounds and come back to me. "Over here Son! Over here!"

No luck.

The other rocks on the shore start to pick up on the crisis of the moment and chime in with sounds of their own. They too, wish to be tossed into the water. They too, remember some of the sounds that the people make. They too, are crying out in despair. They too, have no luck with the Son.

I see Son pick up the other rocks and fling them to the ground in frustration. Daddy offers the Son rocks of his own to no avail. The Son is unhappy and cries out even louder. And louder.

I recognize this sound—loud and clear. It is the same sound the Son made when he picked me up off of the path for the first time. It is the sound of the dream. It is the thirst for the answer. This is a language I know.

I radiate my warmth…

The Son turns around, changes direction, and heads my way. A smile returns to Son's face as he walks on his legs better than I have ever seen him walk before. He takes many more steps in a row than before and cover much more ground.

The rocks around me see the Son coming and make the people sounds louder and louder. I strengthen my resolve and radiate my warmth. Clever rocks, and determined too because they partner with the breeze and roll over the top of me in an attempt to hide me from the Son.

I radiate my warmth…

I can feel the vibrations in the ground as the Son draws closer and the Daddy follows. The vibrations come stronger and stronger still until the Son drops from his legs just above me.
It is dark where I am under these other rocks so I must be hidden from the Son's view.

Warmer and warmer still as I strengthen my resolve. I am glowing with all the dreams and wishes inside me. I know now that the Son will find me. Son will find me because I am a part of him. I am his Special Stone.

Just as the Son is part of his Daddy. And through each other we will all realize our dreams. We will all be able to walk our paths even if we don't have legs; or if our legs don't work so well. Our journeys can become complete if we are willing to include others. Our messages will be heard and understood even if we speak different languages. That is the message inside me. I house that message. And I can deliver that message to a place where the Son and the Daddy can't go. That must be why the Son chose me in the first place. That must be why the Daddy chose his Son.

And that is why I'll reach the water.

That is my belief, my dream. I have faith that it will come true.

Digging and scratching around on the ground, the Son moves the other rocks from view and scoops me up. His hand is warmer than I have ever felt before. The Son has a gleaming look of joy and pride on his face; matching exactly the expression the Daddy has on his face.

In a soft tone, Daddy says, " OK Son, *now* you can make a wish and toss your Special Stone into the water."

The Daddy keeps saying to throw me *into* the water. He means *onto* the water, doesn't he?

The Son smiles even brighter still, his hand so warm now it begins to moisten. He rears back with all his strength and…

flying!
     m   T
     I'   h
     !   e
     a   w
     a   a
     o   t
     o   e
     h   r
     W   i
     .   s
     r   g
     i   e
     a   t
     e   t
     h   i
     t   n
     o   g
     t   c
     n   l
     i   o
     e   s
     m   e
     s   r...
     w
     o
     r   SPLASH !
     h   .
     t
     .   .
     .
     .   .

Chapter 8

Under the Water. Now what?

Splash! I made it to the water! I have made a splash in this world! Or have I? I can't see the surface. I had no idea that there was an entire world below the surface. How do I know that my splash caused a ripple on the surface? Or that those ripples will reach the shores? Did my wish come true? Has my dream been realized?

My dream was to make a splash in this world and I can't tell if I have succeeded or not. I went on this wonderful, scary, exciting, exhilarating journey and I can't even witness the result. That's not fair. I can't even see the Son or the Daddy.
I have to find a meaning to all this because I don't feel good about what just transpired.

I must think back to my journey for the answer. When the Son was thirsty for something to drink, the Daddy walked us down to the water. Once at the shoreline, he put his hands below the surface and scooped something for the Son to drink. That satisfied the Son—he got his answer. Does my answer lie beneath the surface also? Is it surrounding me right now just waiting for me to notice it?

I must believe that all of my efforts have brought me my reward. What if my efforts _were_ the reward? Wow, how about that?

Well, how about that. I learned how to make friends that would help me off the ledge and down to the path. Perfect strangers picked me up and delivered me to the waters' edge. After losing me a number of times, they sought me out and tossed me right into water like I dreamed. All this from a little rock who dreamed of becoming a Special Stone. And all the while, the friends I made who helped get me here all got to learn from me.
Was that my splash? Did I actually teach something to the sun, ice, snow, mud, people, as well as the other rocks? I believe I did!

And now I am floating into this whole new world that I never knew existed. It is a world I know nothing of and recognize even less.

In this new world of wonder, what am I certain of? Only of my dreams and of the gifts I have to offer. Right now this world grows darker and colder as I float downward. It seems as though I'll never know if my splash caused a ripple.

There has to be more than this.

When things got tough in the past, what did I do? What did I believe? Those are the things I must revisit if I am to confirm the result of my journey. It is the language I know best and it has gotten me this far. I must trust it and trust myself that my dreams will light the way.

CHAPTER 9

❦

I Glow; I Know

Sometimes results take time and you don't always see the outcome right away. There were many times during my trip where I had to wait for my efforts to reap a reward. Mother always preached patience. Now may be another opportunity to exercise that virtue.

I am just one small stone, yet I made a huge impact. I made that impact by being me—the very best of me. I had a dream and a burning desire to realize that dream. I tapped into my warmth and dreamed big enough until others joined in to dream along with me. I wasn't the only dreamer in the journey. We attracted each other because in some small way we wanted the same thing. We just did things in our own special way.

So now as I explore my new world, I strengthen my resolve and I radiate my warmth. I dream, even bigger, and I invite others to dream, bigger.

And warmer and warmer still as I strengthen my resolve. I am glowing with all the dreams and wishes inside me. This is what I know—and this language is universal. There is something different this time. I am dreaming of dreams bigger than myself. No longer is this just about what I want to get; or where I want to go. This dream is about what I wish for others.

If I can do it—anybody can do it. Look, I showed you how it's done. Just be the very best of yourself, decide on what you want, and then go for it. Others will join in your quest because their light will shine as well.

As I thought of this, I felt an incredible sense of pride and gratitude. And then something magnificent happened. The water around me warmed up; allowing me to glow once again. As my inner light shined, I began to see reflections all around me, above me and below me.

This world is even busier than the world I came from. There are birds flying all around me, but they have no wings. As I get closer to the ground, I notice all these things walking on the ground. The are not animals, nor are they people. They all seem to have this shell around them—for protection. These things must be like people because people wear a protective shell around them also; people are just better at hiding it.

There are mountains and valleys and paths and caves just like my old world. This world isn't so different after all. The main thing that is unique here is that because of the water, everything down here must learn to communicate with one another—for survival. In this new world, one cannot stand alone and make it, let alone flourish.

As I approach the water's ground, I notice there are many others glowing. Dreamers I suppose. It is a warm and cozy place that I nestle into. My light reflects in all directions, including the surface and beyond. My splash caused a ripple, those ripples formed waves, and those waves found many shores. And that, it seems, is only the beginning.

Oh...my...goodness. And I thought my vantage point from the perch on the mountain was something to behold. From my spot on the mountain looking down, I could see the entire body of water. That was when my big dream started.

From the bottom of the water looking up, I can see the <u>*whole world.*</u>

I dream once again, even bigger.

I invite others once again; to dream, even bigger still...

Chapter 10

❀

Tossing a Stone Each Day

I dreamt big, had faith, and received a wish far greater than I could have ever imagined. There were many times I could have given up. I could have given up on myself, those around me. That definitely would have been the easy thing to do. What I learned from this is that the journey, effort *was* the realization of my dream; it just took me some time to come around to that fact. As a result of my persistence and perseverance, the Son got his wish. Someday he may be the Daddy and bring his Son to these same waters for the same little piece of magic. And that Son bring his Son, and so on.

You see, the magic continues on as long as we make a wish and toss a stone each day. The ripples in the water will always reach shore. And with it they will wash clean another stone to be tossed into the waters. And so the cycle continues.

By the way, that splashing sound you hear is the sound of your greatest wish being answered; and simultaneously your greatest fear being washed away.

Chapter 11

❈

The Beginning...
(Your dream goes here...☺)

Afterword

Well, you have met quite a cast of characters.

These are the stories of *my* characters, what is the story of yours?

Please send me your feedback, your comments, whatever at…

www.milestonesunlimited.com
email…results @milestonesunlimited.com

OK, now turn the light *off* and get some sleep…☺

Best,
Carl Gould

0-595-23315-5